The Pit

DORIS LESSING

A Phoenix Paperback

All stories taken from *London Observed: Stories and Sketches*
published by HarperCollins, 1992 and Flamingo

This edition published in 1996 by Phoenix
a division of Orion Books Ltd
Orion House, 5 Upper St Martin's Lane, London WC2H 9EA

ISBN 1 85799 763 8

Typeset by Deltatype Ltd, Ellesmere Port, Cheshire
Printed in Great Britain by Clays Ltd, St Ives plc

CONTENTS

The Pit   1
What Price the Truth?   36
Two Old Women and a Young One   46

The Pit

Afinal sprig of flowering cherry among white lilac and yellow jonquils, in a fat white jug . . . she stuck this in judiciously, filling in a pattern that needed just so much attention. Shouting 'Spring!' the jug sat on a small table in the middle of the room.

Spring sang in the plane trees that crammed two windows along one wall. The windows of the other wall showed a sprightly blue sky. The trees, full of young leaves, were reflected in the two round mirrors set to match the windows, like portholes in the white wall. Opposite the end wall with its square of blue sky she had hung a large seascape bought for a few pounds in a street market: in it blue sea, blue sky, white spray, white clouds eternally tumbled over each other. It had been painted with a fresh and probably youthful zest by someone called Samantha.

You could think this a large room, extended into infinite variety by the weather outside, but it was small, and so was her bedroom next door. The flat comprised two adequate rooms, and here she had lived for a time.

Having completed preparations for the visit from James, the man to whom she had been married for ten years, she did not sit down, but remained standing by the little table whose surface reflected the flowers. She was giving her room a slow, hooded, prowling look, an inspection not from her viewpoint, but from his. She could not remember his ever actually having criticized her arrangements, but going off with a woman whose taste in every way was the opposite to hers surely must be considered a criticism?

She did not know why he was coming. Two years had passed since she had rung him about some message from Nancy, their daughter, about an urgent need for money. Before that, they had met for lunch, in Manchester as it happened, where she was working and he visiting. In 1980, she thought that was. This encounter had been handled by both of them as if bullets might start flying around the restaurant at a single wrong word, and the strain of it had prevented another. Before that, meetings had always been for legal reasons and policed by solicitors, or because of the children.

But when he had telephoned to say he wanted to meet her 'just to talk', what she had felt, unexpectedly, was delight, as if she were opening a present so well chosen she could feel the giver's thoughts dwelling lovingly among her own, approving her choices.

She perfectly understood the quality of this delight, its exact weight and texture, because of a smile that these days she sometimes felt arriving on her face together with thoughts of certain men. It was a rich, irresponsible, free-booter's smile, and she knew that this smile must appear on their faces when they thought of her: a smile that had nothing to do with what society might be saying at any given time, or with morality, or with the wars between men and women.

But the point was, he – her husband – had not been one of these men, for thoughts of him had been loaded with anxiety and self-doubt. Now she felt that he had been restored to her.

She stood with one capable hand among the reflections of the flowers on the shining tabletop and smiled, not bothering to look in the mirror, for she knew that just as she, meeting him, would seek – anxiously but confidently – among the dry ruins for what she remembered of a quarter of a century ago, so he would seek in her what she had been. This is how former lovers meet, when ageing, as if suffused by that secret, irrepressible smile.

Once upon a time, when young, walking along a pavement or into a room, they had never failed to see in the faces turned towards them the gratified look that comes from absolute rightness. They had been a match, a pair, flesh of an immediately recognizable category of flesh. Both good-looking, healthy, fitted to mate and beget, causing none of the secret unease that people feel when confronted by couples who can make you think only of the unhealthy or ugly offspring they are likely to produce. Sarah and James had given others pleasure that had in fact little to do with being young, handsome, healthy, and so on. No, it was because of their being flesh of one flesh. They had both been tall; she, slim, he, spare. Both were fair, he with shaggy Viking locks, she with long pale gleaming tresses. Both had very blue eyes, full of shrewd innocence. If there ever had been moments of disquiet in their early days, it was because of this: when they lay in each other's arms and looked into that other face, what they saw was so similar to what they saw in mirrors.

The woman he had married after her was large, black-haired, swarthy – a nice change, she had thought, in her bitter days. The children he and this gypsy had made between them were 'one white and one black and two khaki', as she had put it, full of shame. (Not literally 'black' of course: one was like her mother, brown and sleek and dark-eyed; one like James, pale and fair with eyes that shocked because of their blueness; and two indeterminate beings like neither.) Nice-looking children, but when these six people were all together no one need think of them as a family.

When Sarah and James were together, with their two children, they were four of a kind, blue-eyed, blond Northern Europeans, so different from the majority of the world's people that you had to think this was some kind of a rare and threatened race and you were being privileged to see perfect representatives of it. She had not seen things like this then, but later she did, confronted with Rose and the new family.

The two children were now, of course, more than grown up. One was in Boston. This was Nancy with her husband and children. The son was on some island in the Pacific investigating the ways of fish. She did not often see either of them, or her grandchildren. She was pretty sure this was because of the divorce happening when it did, when they were ten and eleven. Protecting themselves, they had separated inwardly not only from their father, who had betrayed them for the new family, but from her, the innocent party. They had become cautious, sparing of affection, self-doubting, and critical. Of her. Unjust! But these days she never used, or thought, words like justice, or happiness.

When her Viking husband had left her for the siren-voiced, histrionic, over-colourful Rose, she had – of course! – been devastated. Literally. She fell apart. Well, women did. She was for a time poisoned with bitterness, she could not believe that her husband, her *friend*, had so treated her. Oh no, it was not possible: she confronted him with the impossibility of it, the indignant innocence of her gaze demanding an explanation she could acknowledge. She drank too much. Then she stopped drinking. She coped well and sensibly with the two sensible and over-cautious children who, like her, protected a calloused place.

But all that had gone away, seemed to belong to some other time, even some other woman.

Now she felt herself connected, not with that vulnerable discarded woman, but with herself as a girl, before she had met him.

Deliverance from weakness had not happened quickly. Five years after the divorce, at a party, he had stared at her, as if unable to believe what his eyes and senses told him, that this was – still – his wife, with whom he had lived for ten years. The tears spilled down his face, and he exclaimed, 'But Sarah, what happened?' At which she had been so angry she spat at him (astonishing herself as well as him – it was behaviour she associated with gypsy women, never her moderate self) and turned her back on him and left the party, weeping. But other women had told her that on

5

unexpectedly meeting former husbands, these men would also exclaim, genuinely startled, 'But what happened?' As if their delinquency was something not only surprising to them, but not really their responsibility at all, rather the result of some ineluctable fate.

For a while, she had raged over what she had then seen as the lying sentimentality of 'But what happened?' Had raged briefly, because one did *not* permit self-indulgence in useless emotion. And then had forgotten, it had all gone away, and when she thought of him, not often these days, what she saw was the blue innocence of that look of his, reflecting the candour and honesty that she had first loved in him, qualities she prized above all others.

Now she lived in her two adequate rooms. In the same town as he did – but that was chance. Because of her work she had lived in Paris, New York, various towns in England, always moving, and good at moving. She never felt she lived in one place more than another. She was a personal secretary in a big oil firm.

But her husband had left her for that other house where he had lived, not moving at all, with his new family. Not always contentedly, as she knew. But she did not now care about all that. He had made his bed, and she genuinely hoped it was a good one. She did not care, one way or the other. Not to care, that was the great, the unexpected, the miraculous deliverance. What a lot of nonsense it all was, the anguish, and the suffering, and the lying awake at nights weeping! What a waste of time.

And now when she was free of him, James was coming to see her.

His footsteps approached. Rapidly. Lightly. He was taking two steps at a time up the stairs, then he knocked, and was in, standing just inside the door and looking at her.

Knowing exactly how they must look to each other, they frowned with the effort of re-creating younger selves in what they were actually seeing. Their eyes met without difficulty, and did not disengage because of confusion, pain, guilt. Perhaps they had not really seen each other since the separation.

What was she looking at was an elderly Viking, his shaggy locks, like hers, tarnished with silver. He was much burned by sun, wind, so there must have been a very recent walking holiday somewhere. His handsome face was thin, all crags and ravines. He seemed to have dried out, as she seemed to herself to be dry and light, time dragging moisture out of her, like a sun.

His acute gaze now left her, and rested on the flowers . . . a small table where she took her meals . . . a gas fire with a light armchair beside it . . . a shelf of books . . . the tumultuous blue and white seascape. Then he approached the blue square of the end window, with his fast light high step that had been the first thing in him to delight her. It still did. At the window he looked downward into a scene of back gardens, birds, trees, fences loaded with creepers, children's climbing frames, cats stretched out absorbing sunlight. Family life . . . He was scrutinizing it with a small dry smile she knew well. Then he stepped quickly to one window in the side wall, and then the other: the same view from both; a quiet street lined with parked cars, plane trees, an old woman sitting on a bench.

This was the second floor. In summer the trees were like towns full of birds, and she stood there watching them. He turned about, and stood checked in his need to step off to somewhere else in this room. He was used to rooms where one might walk about, take a short stroll. But there was nowhere else. He was feeling confined.

'I suppose you are wondering what I'm doing here?' he said hastily, but then went red, because it sounded conventional, though she had not taken it like that.

'Well, yes, I did wonder,' she said agreeably, and sat herself down near the flowers. She at once became conscious of how she must look, posed near these flowers she had bought because of pleasure at his coming, and she moved quickly to the armchair near the gas fire. It was a chair that made one sit up straight. She sat there lightly and erectly, and looked at him. And sighed. She heard the sigh, and saw his quick conscious look when he heard it, and it was her turn to blush.

He sat down near one of the windows and beyond him a plane tree shook with the visitations of birds. He looked as if he might leap to his feet and be off again. A hunted man, he frowned, and put his lean brown hand to his face, but then let it drop and sighed too, and sat back in his chair to face her.

'There isn't a reason really,' he announced. 'It began to seem to me so wrong, that we didn't even meet occasionally.'

She merely smiled, agreeing that they had not met only because of some whim or oversight.

'We were together all that time . . . the children . . .' He shrugged, giving up, and looked straight at her, inviting aid.

She could, she supposed, ask after his children, his other family. But there was no point in his coming, no point in all this upset and adjustment and sighing and excitement if all they did was to exchange pretexts for not talking. Besides, she knew how they all were, his family: a good friend of hers remained a good friend of his, and reported what went on. Not like a spy, but like a friend. Once she had needed to know; recently she had listened as if to news from a household that did not much concern her.

He half got up, but sat down again, seeing there was nowhere to move to. 'You don't have much space up here,' he remarked. It sounded like a reproach, and he again reddened.

'But I don't need much space.' And now this, she felt, could be taken as a reproach, and she made an irritable gesture – too irritable for what was happening, full of elderly impatience at the trivial. 'I didn't mean . . .' she exclaimed carefully, 'what I meant was, I *don't* need much room, now the children are grown up. Nancy and Martin hardly need their own rooms any longer!'

Suddenly he seemed tired. She knew why. The house he now lived in was large, full of rooms in which one might take a little stroll. But it was of course always needing repairs the way houses did, and it was shabby, because it was a much used family house, exploding with the four children and their friends. It pulsated with people, noise, music, telephones ringing, loud voices – Rose's, particularly – singing, a dog barking, doorbells, the drone of vacuum cleaners. Family life. The oldest child was fifteen, the 9 youngest, nine. In front of James was at least ten years, probably much more, of finding a good deal of money for education. He was a business consultant. He had not wanted to be one. But that was what he had become when, needing a lot of money for the new marriage, he had given up his previous career as an expert in electronics for the aircraft industry and for boats. That was what he had enjoyed.

Everything he did now, where he lived and how, was because he had fallen in love with Rose, her own opposite in every way, and gone off with her. And things would go on as they were now, they would have to, for years and years. He was fifty-three. He would grow old in Rose's service. That was what he had chosen. If you could use a word like 'choose'.

She was two years older than he.

She said, 'I decided to retire this year. They asked me to stay on, but I don't want to.'

And now his whole person was momentarily full of the energy of words not spoken, words of aggressive inquiry, if not reproach. It was he who had arranged her very good job with the oil firm. He knew – since the man she had worked for all these years was a friend – that pressure had been put on her to be more than a personal secretary. They had offered her all kinds of better jobs. But she had not wanted to become ambitious and sink her life in the firm's. She had found her own life more interesting, and had been careful to guard it. But had she accepted, money would have been much less tight. She knew of course that James had been critical of her for being content to be a mere secretary, and this quite apart from the money side of it.

She said, 'I don't need very much money now. I can do as I please.'

'Lucky Sarah,' he said, suddenly emotional.

'Yes, I think so.'

'There is no way, no way at *all* that I could *not* have gone off with Rose,' he said unexpectedly. Unexpectedly to him: but she knew this was why he had come. He had to say this! Not as a justification. Not as a plea. He needed to explain some absolute, some imperative, that she – his first wife – must acknowledge. He was asking for justice. From her!

'No, I know,' she said judicially.

'It was like . . .' He hesitated, and not from delicacy, or wanting to spare her, or himself, but because of the astonishment even now: his face was contracted with the effort of coming to terms with what he remembered. 'I don't understand it,' he said. 'I didn't then. I never have. I could even say I didn't like her particularly . . .' His look at her insisted she must not take this as disloyalty to Rose, or an excuse.

'I know,' she said again.

'It was because . . . but I simply had to . . . it was like being carried away by a . . .'

Now she made a sharp irritable gesture, meaning *That's enough*. But he did not see it, or if he did, decided to ignore it.

'Have you ever thought, Sarah . . . we are so alike, we two . . .'

She nodded.

His eyes had filled with tears, and it was because of his 11 bewilderment.

'From one extreme to the other,' he said. 'We never had to explain anything, did we? We always understood . . . but with her, it's like a wrong turning in a foreign country, and I don't know the language.' A silence. 'The dark and the light of it,' he said. A silence. 'I am not saying I regret it. You don't regret what you couldn't help. Or if you do it's a waste of time.'

'Of course not,' she agreed.

And now he did get up and stand before her, hands dangling, but with their characteristic look of being on the alert and ready for anything. An embrace? But he went instead to the end window, whose blue square now showed a fat and cherubic cloud, white with gold and fawn shadows. He looked at the cloud, over the disordered back gardens.

'What are you going to do, Sarah?'

'I want to travel.'

'But you're always on the move. Every time I hear of you, you're somewhere else,' he said, with the short laugh that means suppressed envy.

'Yes, I've been lucky. It's been a lovely job, thanks to you. But they say elderly women get restless feet, and that's what I've got.'

'Not only women,' he said, but shut off the complaint with, 'Are you going to visit Nancy and Martin?'

'Briefly.'

He looked an inquiry.

'I would not describe us as a close family,' she said, and he reddened again.

'Well, I think perhaps we are. Rose is good at that, making a family, I mean.'

At this, resentment nearly overwhelmed her. She knew he had never understood what it had been like for her, the years of bringing up the children without him. He never would. She maintained a smiling silence. But now she felt at a distance with him, because of his not understanding.

'Anyway, it wasn't such a bad thing,' he said. 'They saw all those different places with you moving about so much, and they were in different schools and fit in anywhere.'

'Citizens of the world,' she said dryly. 'That's what they are, all right.'

He could have taken this up, pressing his point, which was necessary to him. But she stopped it with, 'I shall begin by going on walking tours here. In this country first. I mean, real long ones, all summer . . .'

'Ah yes,' he said energetically, 'there's nothing like it.'

'And then I shall go walking in France and Germany, well, everywhere I can in Europe. Norway . . .'

'Ah yes,' he said, restless, his feet moving as if ready to set off then and there.

Rose did not like walking.

'Around the world,' she said. 'Why not?' And she laughed, her whole body, her face, alive with delight at the thought of it, setting off free as a bird . . . No, that was wrong, birds were not free, they had to obey all kinds of patterns and forces – free as only a human being can be. Though, probably, life being what it was, free only for a short, treasured time before something or other happened. Free to walk, stop, make friends, wander, change her mind, 13 sit all day on a mountainside if she felt like it, watching clouds . . . She had actually forgotten that he stood there, watching her, smiling his appreciation of her.

'Sarah,' he said, in a low intimate voice, with the thrill of recklessness in it, 'why can't we two go off again somewhere, this summer, soon . . .'

The two smiled at each other, as if their faces were a few inches apart on a pillow. Then she heard herself sigh, and she saw the energy go out of him.

'But why not, Sarah?' he urged.

This meant that what Olive had told her was true. Rose was having an affair, and he did not feel bound to be loyal.

'You mean, Rose wouldn't mind?'

The thought of how much Rose would mind, and how she would show it, was obviously like a blow to the back of his knees, for he sank down abruptly, and stared, not at her, Sarah, but at the cloud, which now seemed sculptured out of honey-coloured stone.

'Or you wouldn't tell her?' she persisted.

Going off with her on a walking tour was an impulse. He had not thought of it before he came, or not seriously. But probably he would not have felt free to come, if Rose had not set him free. Quid pro quo . . . well, that is how *he* would see it.

Serious, brought down, he looked straight at her, to avoid accusations of evasion, and said, 'I would have to tell her. She would find out anyway. She would know.'

'Yes, she would.'

'But why not, Sarah? Why ever not? There must be limits to being a good . . . provider.'

What he had been going to say she didn't know. A good husband? A good father?

What she was thinking was: living with Rose has softened your brain. This is the kind of thing she goes in for, having your cake and eating it and pretending nothing has happened.

'Look, why don't we two go to Scotland? You remember all that, Sarah?'

They had been on a three weeks' walking tour in Scotland, just before they married in 1958.

'We could go next month,' he urged. 'I've got three weeks due.'

She shut her eyes, remembering the two of them walking up a heather-covered mountainside.

'Sarah,' she heard, gruff, accusing, 'I've been thinking about so much. There's such a terrible gap in my life. There has been, for years.'

She said dryly, eyes still shut, 'Polygamy! You'd like that!' But she was smiling, she could not stop.

'Yes, yes,' he shouted, and reached her in two long strides. 'Yes, if that's what it is, *yes*.'

The little armchair by the fire had no companion, and he reached out a long arm and pulled across a chair in which he sat, close beside her. He put his arm around her.

'Sarah,' he crooned, his cheek on hers. 'Sarah,' he went on saying, while their cheeks glued themselves together with tears.

Suddenly the little room dazzled and glared. A sunbeam hitting a windowpane had been reflected onto a mirror just above their heads, and this in turn sent lozenges and prisms of colour onto a wall. Now it was like sitting in a pool of glittering water, submerging furniture, flowers, and themselves.

She freed herself from him, got up, pulled curtains across the end window. The curtains were white and unlined. That wall was now flat and white-shadowed, with a large rectangle where hot orange pricked through. Part of this rectangle lifted, and a tangerine-coloured sail swelled out into the room and subsided. In a few moments the sunlight would cease to beat against the back of the curtains, and the whole wall would be a dead flat white.

Their mood had quite changed.

She did not dare go and sit by him again. If she did, she would sink into . . . into . . .

He was gazing at her through the warm orange light that soaked everything.

'Sarah?' he inquired, as if searching for her in a maze.

He stood up, said, 'All the same, why not, Sarah? I don't see one good rational reason why not! I want you in my life! I need you! I simply cannot do without you.'

He came to her, bent, and gently rubbed his cheek against hers: it was a husband's, not a lover's, claim.

And then he was off, and she heard him bounding down the stairs.

The room was dimming. The glare behind the curtains no longer delineated every thread of the coarse linen. The shrill warning clatter of the birds in the plane tree was an evening sound, not the companionable gossiping of the day. The light abruptly faded off the curtains. That wall was now uninterruptedly white.

She sat down in the chair by the flowers. She looked at them critically. The jug was too smug, too contented a round shape for the gawky, stiff awkwardness of the cherry and the fresh spring lilac with its loose random flowers. She moved the jug to the floor behind her, and tried to think.

She was in a boil of emotions that were resolving into a single need: to escape . . . run away, in fact. Run, run, run out of this room, this building, out of London, yes, out of England. She was now out of her chair, and moving clumsily and fast about the room, like a shut-in bird. But what on earth was all this about? She had to run away from James, was that it? But this meeting of theirs had nothing of threat in it; on the contrary, for it had seemed as if some spell had been taken off them that until now had made every meeting, even a telephone call, an angry, guilty, embarrassed misery. Being with James today had been more like the first meeting of people who are going to love each other, full of recognitions and sweet surprises. But her heart was pounding, her stomach hurt, and she was being ravaged by anxiety.

She forced herself to sit down again, composing her limbs to suit her position, that of an elderly lady considering her situation with sober common sense. She was eyeing the telephone, she observed, as if her nerves expected it to ring, and unpleasantly.

If James had gone straight home, and if Rose was at home, then of course something about him would instantly have alerted her, even if he had not said at once – which was more likely – 'I've just been talking to Sarah, oh no, don't 17 worry, I just dropped in on an impulse, that's all, nothing more to it.' She could positively hear him saying it.

Crisis could easily have taken over that house. Rose would already be on the telephone to her current confidante. She had one at a time, in an intense and dramatic bond, full of intimate meetings and vibrant conversations, but then there would be a quarrel, and another ex-intimate of whom she would say, 'I'm not going *there* if I'm likely to meet *her*, the cow!' She might at this very moment be saying to whoever it was, 'My God! Do you know what has happened? I'm losing my husband, that's all! He's started seeing his first wife – yes, Sarah! For God's sake, I've *got* to talk about it, it's urgent. No, cancel it! Come at once, please . . .'

While waiting for this tête-à-tête, which would be the first of very many, several a day, Rose would be laying out the cards, consulting *I Ching*, and making an appointment with her fortune-teller, a woman of limitless psychological penetration who was as familiar with her (Sarah's) life, as she was with Rose's; she (Sarah) had been pronounced of no threat to Rose; but her type, the Fair Lady, standing in opposition to Rose as Dark Lady, was, and always would be.

Rose lived in terror of some slim blonde nymphet. By the time the confidante arrived, Fate would already have pronounced through several mouths, or at least have given some pretty definite indications. As a result of the meeting between the two women all kinds of things would start to happen. The first, that her telephone (Sarah's) would start to ring. Someone she had never heard of would be saying,

'Do forgive me for bothering you, but I believe you can help me, actually James suggested it. Can you tell me something about Manchester? You were there, he said? You had a house there, didn't you? What are the schools like?'

Yes, James would know this call was going to be made, for Rose would have said in an airy, confident way, challenging James with a bold, laughing look, 'Oh, James, Sarah could advise, couldn't she? She knows all about Manchester!' All kinds of telephone calls and even happenings, none of them unreasonable, and on the face of it the essence of civilized good sense. Just like James coming to see her this afternoon. On the face of it . . .

Telephone calls from another of Rose's best friends – like a schoolgirl she only had best friends – 'Oh, Sarah, do you remember me, we met at the Tillings', do you remember? I hear you are going off with James to Wales? If you are going anywhere near Swansea, would you drop in and see an old friend of mine, she's so lonely these days since her husband died, she would be more than happy to put you both up, it would be such a kindness.'

Soon, a telephone call from Rose herself. The low, vibrant voice, always hinting at things that simply could not be said. 'Sarah, this is Rose! Yes, Rose! I've been wanting to really get to know you for such a long time . . . Do you think we could meet and have a real talk? No, I've discussed it all with James, and he'd love it. Would you invite me to tea? I'd love to see your flat, James says it's so pretty. Oh, I'd love to live in a flat, just by myself, just to be free, and *myself*, you understand?'

There would be many other telephone calls from Rose,

casual, offhand, insulting. 'Sarah, is James there? No, but I thought . . . oh, I must have been mistaken. If he does drop in, do tell him to ring me, there's been a bit of a crisis, he's got to deal with it.'

While all this went on, Rose would be saying to absolutely everyone, 'I'm sorry to say there's a crisis in my marriage. James and I are both working at it, we have been so happy, and I'm sure it will all be right in the end.'

Her love affair would have been given up, after many weepy meetings. 'I have to make a choice, my darling love. Oh it isn't easy . . . the children . . .'

People would in fact be expecting the marriage to end. It was Rose's fourth. Her story, as far as it could be ascertained, for it changed with whomever she was telling it to, was something like this. She had emerged from the miseries of Europe after the war having already experienced everything in the way of hunger, of cold, and the threat of death. Her mother had died in a concentration camp, in some versions, but in others she had abandoned Rose for a lover. Rose, who was very pretty, married an American in the occupying force, whom she had madly loved, though some people knew, without condemning her, that she had become this man's mistress because if one wanted to eat, one had to attach oneself to one of the new armies.

Then she married another American, much better placed than the first. But she said she hated America, which was why she married an Englishman who was important in the oil empires of the world. He had adored her, this exotic clever waif, but he did not adore her long. He was reputed to have said that he should have refused to marry her, and kept her as a mistress. She would never be a wife. It was like having a beautiful spoiled pet in the house, something like a cheetah, that couldn't be house-trained. That marriage had lasted three years.

Rose had done some serious thinking, and taken the advice of her fortune-teller. She was already well into her thirties. Married to James she had been a real wife, a good one, presiding over comfort and good meals, with one satisfactory baby after another. These were in themselves evidence of remarkable strength of mind, for everyone knew she had had 'dozens' of abortions and miscarriages. Each pregnancy, and then birth, had claimed the attention not only of James, midwives, doctors, hospitals, friends, neighbours, but circles of people who had scarcely heard of Rose, so remarkable and unprecedented did it turn out to be.

Sarah had contemplated these dramas with dislike, with distaste, and, above all, with incredulity that James could tolerate it all. One simply did not make a fuss about physical suffering (or any suffering if it came to that); one shut up, kept a stiff upper lip, bit the bullet, et cetera and so forth. Forced by Rose to examine these tenets, this *English* creed, Sarah concluded there was nothing wrong with it, and there was no virtue at all in all these foreign histrionics which, in Rose's case, were always compounded with dishonesty, with calculations so devious that sometimes it was years later before one understood what had really been going on.

21

Quite soon after inviting herself to tea, Rose was going to ring up and say something like this: 'Sarah! Yes, it's me, it's Rose! Sarah, I wonder if you would come to dinner? No, oh, don't say you won't without thinking about it. Why not, Sarah? We have so many friends in common, not to mention James, oh no, I don't mean that badly, I swear I don't, Sarah, oh, do believe me . . .'

She could see herself, one of several guests around that capacious family table, James at one end, Rose at the other, the children eyeing the adults as her own two had done her: polite, even deferential towards these appalling and cruel inevitabilities, but with nervous glances at each other, with wide, scared smiles. They would eat quickly and make excuses to leave the table and go to their rooms, where they would sit and discuss fearfully, angrily, but full of loud derision (because of their fear) the dangerous situation downstairs. 'Our father's first wife has come to supper . . . Sarah, oh don't you know about Sarah? Well, she's here for supper. Can I come over to your house?' So they would talk on the telephone to some friend.

Soon after this civilized and creditable-to-everyone family supper, James would say, with that resentful but admiring laugh he used to meet the situations Rose put him into, 'Sarah, Rose suggested we should take the two older children with us when we go off to France. They are very good at walking, you know. I took them to the Lake District last year. Would you mind?'

She would say she didn't mind. And probably she wouldn't. By then she would have become great friends with all the children, and a lot of her time would be taken up in choosing them presents and all the votive offerings children do need these days. She would have become – not a second mother, Rose would see to that – but a nice auntie, to all the children. She would say to James, 'How nice to have Sam and Betty along. What a pity the other two aren't old enough to come too, but perhaps next year. Of course I don't mind their coming. Why not?'

Except that her heart beat, her palms were itchy with sweat, and she was again prowling around the room as if preparing to leap through a window and into the street and be off – to anywhere at all.

What power that woman had! Always!

It was the strength of unscrupulousness, rooted in selfishness, and born from – stupidity. It had never, ever, occurred to Rose that one should *not* do this or that. (But of course there was the question of that childhood in the camps. Did this mean that one would never, ever, judge Rose by ordinary standards?) During Sarah's bad time, when she had thought, much too much, about Rose, she had always come up against this, like running headlong into a glass barrier that stood between Rose and the rest of the world. To say to Rose, 'But one can't do that, don't you see?' To say, 'But that's not the decent thing to do!' – why, even in imagination when it is easy to see oneself saying this and that to an antagonist, the words simply would not get themselves formed.

But ... stupidity? If it was that, then it got Rose everything. Sarah's husband. Four children. A large house. Stability after being flotsam. A man whose life was captive to her needs. Stupidity! No, it was a force, a power, that   23 came from some level of human existence Sarah had never entered. When she had watched James go off to Rose, she had felt exactly as she would had she seen him, in a dream, pulled into a bewitched forest governed by primitive laws. She had felt he was leaving his own best self.

But then, there were the children. Over and over again during those years she had said to herself, 'Sarah, there are four children. Four children, Sarah. You can't argue with that.' Every child brings with it the unknown, brings possibilities and chances rooted in the distant past of humanity, possibilities stretching away into the future. James might have gone off into the enchanted forest after a witch, but there he had found four packages addressed to himself, each one full of Fate.

She supposed that Rose was James's *anima*, embodying a whole parcel of attributes that James's daylight self most deeply needed. She could see there was no fighting that.

It was Rose's fortune-teller who had said Rose was James's *anima*. And where had Sarah's comparable male been? Often enough Sarah had dwelled, but no more than adequately, on the two men with whom she had had affairs after James left her. Affairs are not easy, with adolescent children already sensitized to be on the watch for wrong-doing, not easy when you are holding down a job, and having to move to this or that town or country to keep it, always juggling children, their needs, term times, holidays, flats, houses, travelling. Her two affairs had been pleasant enough, if harassed and circumscribed by all these prob-lems, and indeed the men in question put that rich relishing smile on her face whenever she thought of them. But she did not believe they represented any more than themselves.

No, it was James, she believed, who embodied that man who was her imperative, her other self. But there seemed to be an imbalance somewhere in the psychological equation. Often enough she had tried to picture some dark, dramatic, vibrant *lying* man who would silence all her best instincts, but she had concluded at last that this force could only be female. (She did not like this conclusion because she was a feminist.) She could not imagine a man with Rose's attributes. She had never met one, or even read about one. A man like Rose would be degenerate, or criminal.

But Rose was not degenerate or criminal. She was simply – female. Of a certain type that every woman at once and instinctively recognized at first sight. And every man had to respond to, at once, either with attraction, or unease and dislike. No man was ever indifferent to Rose.

Rose had only to walk into a room . . .

Ten years after she and James had married, ten happy years – and James always made a point of granting that, being fair, decent, and honourable – the two of them went to a party together. They had got there late because of some problem with a baby-sitter.

In the middle of a room stood a couple, a dark dramatic-looking woman, and a very young man. He was a boy, really, a poetic English boy, like Rupert Brooke. She was fascinating him. He was hypnotized by her. She was tall and slender, though this could hardly be discerned under swirling draperies, for she wore a gown made out of a scarlet, silver-broidered sari. Her black glistening hair snaked down her shoulders and back. One strand lay on a slim brown arm, and – this was Sarah's immediate, sardonic observation – this seductive coil was being kept there on sleek and shining skin by an angle of that arm, the elbow lifted, making a tender, poignant curve. Rose was not beautiful, but everyone was looking at her; and at the poor young man, kept helpless by the black depths of her eyes.

Sarah was indignant that the youth was being used in this way. Rose was sending out sly swift glances to the men who were watching, to judge her effect on them, and glances of connivance at the women who, and she would never ever understand this, were hating her for it, and would not send back equal glances. 'Look what a fool I am making of this poor male sucker,' was what she expected all the women present to share. Sarah looked at James, counting on him to feel what she felt, but she saw that his look at Rose was like the young man's. He was already lost with his first view of Rose, while his good wife Sarah was engaged at feeling ashamed for her sex at its worst. What Sarah was thinking at the very moment her husband was losing his senses, his good sense, was, 'She's *female*, she's female in a basic gutter way that every decent woman in the world hates.'

He walked straight over to Rose. People looked at Sarah standing there, abandoned, for she had been: nothing could have been more blatant. The poor poetic youth, forgotten from that moment, stumbled to one side as James took his place. And that was how Sarah had lost her husband to Rose, as simply and as inevitably as that. When the time came to go home, she touched him on the arm, and he came away from Rose with whom he had been talking for three hours, not looking at his wife or at anyone else.

She took the bemused man home, and he came to the same bed, and he lay awake, and so did she, listening to how he sighed and suffered, and there was a moment towards morning, the early light already in the room, when he said, 'But Sarah, what happened? I don't understand. Did I behave badly?'

Everyone in that room knew what had happened. That very next morning Olive, the couple's great friend, rang up Sarah and said, 'Forget it, there's nothing you can do, it'll have to run its course.'

And 'it' was still running its course.

'It' was about to engulf her too.

'Sarah,' said Sarah to herself, as elderly people do. 'Sarah, do you realize you are thinking of actually running away? Running out of this flat, which you like, from this city, which you love, simply to get away from Rose, get away from. . . ?

'No, come on, surely you are exaggerating. Suppose you do exactly what James suggests, neither more nor less. You will go off with him for three weeks on a walking trip (and what you are imagining now is the delight, not of lovemaking, but of talking, talking with someone who perfectly understands you, your other self), and it doesn't matter where you go – Scotland, Timbuktu. You will of course insist that Rose should be told, for that is the decent and honourable thing to do. You will *not* respond to her telephone calls, but simply be polite, no more, nor to the indirect telephone calls, each one of which will have the unmistakable flavour of Rose's deviousness. You will not become a guest at Rose's table, or a kind auntie to her children – part, in short, of Rose's life, her family, that *quicksand*. You will simply go off with James for a walking holiday and that is that! All simple and aboveboard.'

Sarah sank down in her little straightbacked armchair and closed her eyes. She was being absurd. Even to begin to think like this meant she was already sucked in.

'No,' she would have to tell James. 'No, no, no, James, it simply will not do, you must see that.' He would have seen it at once, if he had not spent fifteen years with Rose.

Even before the telephone rang she was staring at it as if it was about to explode.

Cautiously she lifted the handpiece and said, 'Yes?'

A child's voice.

'Is that Sarah?' said a little girl (Betty, probably, in a breathless voice that had in it, already, all of Rose's shamelessness).

'Yes,' said Sarah.

'Is my father there?'

'No,' said Sarah.

Prompted by Rose, the child said, 'Thank you,' and the line went dead.

Sarah was standing by the telephone in a dark room, and the two tall side windows showed tenebrous branches against a hazy sky. She was weakened already. She was unable to prevent thoughts of what it would be like with James back in her life. Good Lord, how much he had taken with him, when he left her for Rose! And now, how easy not to go away (*run* away, she was fiercely accusing herself);

how easy to stay and see it through to the end.

The end? Why the *end*?

Sarah switched on the lights, and stood in a small bright room, the night shut away from her. She was breathing fast, her whole being prickling with some kind of energy . . . it was hard to keep still, she was striding around that room of hers, so much too small for her. She saw in one of the little mirrors a distressed, wild-looking creature with distracted eyes, and with moving lips, too. She was muttering to herself, this woman, this Sarah – herself.

She was muttering, 'It's not me, it's her. Not Sarah, Rose.'

What did she mean by that . . . 'What *is* it?' she demanded of herself irritably. 'What is the matter?' For she felt as if she was being invaded by some understanding that was like a powerful substance, changing her. 'Rose, it's Rose. Not me, but Rose.' These words were on her lips forcing her to attend to them.

She switched off the lights again and stood by the window in the end wall. The disorder of the gardens was hidden by the dark, and all she could see were roofs against the sky.

She shut her eyes. She breathed slowly. She was seeing (the picture forced itself on her, the fragile arms of a young girl stretching upward out of some kind of pit, or trap. Golden brown arms, with a fine sheen of dark hair . . . the child's fingers reached up, closed on the edge of the pit, and then big boots came crunching down, and the arms fell back but crept up again, and tenacious fingers clutched at the loose soil that crumbled as she tried to hold it. The delicate

29

arms tensed there, trembling . . .). Sararh shut her eyes so as not to see the big boots come stamping down.

How had pretty young girls got themselves out of all that . . . how had they survived?

Sarah was a child in the war, and while it went on her view of it was the conventional one presented to her by the necessities of wartime. Her father was in the Air Force. After the war both parents were involved with helping refugees out of the shambles that was Europe. Sarah had known about 'all that'. But without knowing about it. Still a child she had told herself, 'Of course one can't really understand what it is like, all that, not if one is English.' Meaning, 'not if you've been safe all your life.' (And will go on being safe, was implicit.) 'All that' was a horror outside ordinary living, and there was no point dwelling on it, because if one hadn't been in it, one would never understand. Sarah had closed a door in herself. Rather, she had refused to open it. And yes, she believed she was right to do it. One needn't allow oneself to wallow in horrors.

When she had first heard Rose's history she had listened and kept the door shut. For one thing she did not believe it. Yes, she knew Rose had been there, had escaped from 'all that'. Not necessarily, however, in the way she said. Rose was a liar. She lied as she breathed. Rose was one of those people who, if they say they walked up a street on the right side going east, one automatically corrected it to 'the left side, going west'.

Rose had been – so she had told some people – in a concentration camp. Had told others, more than one. Her mother had died in a camp. Her father was a fabulously rich South American who had had this amazing love affair with her beautiful mother, but he was married and had gone back to his wife. True? Who knew! (Who cared, Sarah had added, in moments of moral exhaustion. There was always too much of Rose!)

Sarah knew that a lot of people who had emerged from 'all that' said they were in camps, and perhaps they had been, but the words stood for a horror that people who had not been part of 'all that' did not have to enter. Could not enter. A kind of shorthand, that's what these words were . . . the camps had only been part of it. They were a black pit into which people were sucked, or thrown, or fell, but around it people had struggled and fought to save themselves, save others, in ways that no outsider could imagine. Rose had emerged from 'all that', and if her stories weren't true, what of it?

She had come out. She had survived. That was enough.

She had three times been the petted, petulant, child-wife, mistress-wife, of adoring men who had got rid of her because she could not fit herself into being ordinary, being a wife.

How had she seen that? She had played a part she had to believe in, because it brought her out of the black pit, because it had saved her, but then it hadn't been appropriate after all. She had then decided to become a good wife, all home-made bread and noisy children in a family house. But she had had to make the decision to be that. This Rose, the good wife of James, was a construct, a role, just as the other, the petted, pretty, child-mistress had been.

31

Rose had never understood this world, the safe, ordered world, which was not 'all that'. She had never ever been able to grasp the rules that governed it. Yes, they were mostly unwritten rules, and yes of course one absorbed them as one grew up, the way Sarah had.

Rose had not.

Sarah stood by the window in a dark room with her eyes shut, and her perspectives had so far changed that she was almost Rose, she was feeling with her. And what she felt (Sarah now knew, in her own bones and flesh) was panic. Fear was the air Rose breathed. She was like someone continually reaching out for hand-holds that seemed solid but gave way. Three husbands, married for safety, had crumbled in her hands, leaving her desperate, determined to find – James.

And now James, this marriage, was giving way.

This love affair (with another poetic young Englishman, so Sarah had heard) was another face of panic – middle-aged Rose was trying to reassure herself that she could still attract.

Sarah began replaying in her mind the scenes she foretold earlier.

Rose, frantic, desperate, distraught with fear, on the telephone to a 'best friend', who she had to know by now would suddenly cease to be a friend, because Rose was too much, because of her excessiveness. 'I have too much vitality, too much energy for the English!' she would complain, while those great black eyes of hers looked inward, full of incomprehension, wondering what she had done *this* time. You have been lying again, Sarah told

Rose's image. But Rose would never understand what Sarah meant. Rose lied as she breathed about absolutely everything, but for her this was just survival, it was what had saved her, had got her out of the horrible place that was her childhood. Rose wove nets around James, that he would never understand, just as she could never understand him.

Rose would never, ever, understand ordinary decency, common sense, honesty. One did not learn these qualities when part of 'all that'.

Weaving nets and snares, crazy with fear, using every trick she knew, she would pull her rival Sarah towards her, into that house, that family, and then . . . The great family table with the children around it, and their friends. James at the head of the table, and sometimes his colleagues. She, Rose, at its foot. Olive . . . other people . . . And there, too, Sarah, sitting modestly in her place at the side of the table, with the children, like a visitor. Her husband (Rose's) with his first wife, the two Northerners, two elderly Vikings, handsome if sun- and wind-dried, humorous, judicious, not commenting on this scene, and not even allowing their eyes to meet (which in itself would be enough to drive Rose hysterical with suspicion for she always and with everyone used those great eyes of hers in glances, connivings, little raisings of the brow, dark meaningful looks – she could not manage without them! Had never managed without them, her atmosphere of me-and-you) . . . but there they sat, her husband and Sarah, calm, smiling, undramatic, and at home in a world that Rose did not understand, and could not, for she had been born into that other place, where people survived.

Rose could do not other than weave nets around Sarah, using James to do it. She would plot and plan and intrigue, lay snares for the world she could not understand, and she would pull it into her life and into her home and sit it at her table.

And then?

And then she would kill herself. There was nothing else for her. Her panic, her horror, would not be assuaged, appeased, because Sarah, obedient, amenable, sat at her table, but, on the contrary, it would rise up in her and kill her.

Of course!

It was obvious!

It had been obvious from the start, and that was why Sarah had been in such a panic herself. To get out . . . to get away . . . to make sure none of these things would happen.

'Rose, not Sarah.' 'Her, not me,' she had heard herself muttering, from the part of her (that part of us all) which was so much more intelligent than the slow, lumbering, daylike self.

Rose would ring herself, tonight. Or another of the children would. Or James would, with a message from Rose.

Sarah would simply not answer the telephone.

Meanwhile she switched on the lights, found a certain letter in a drawer, and dialled her old friend Greta in Norway. 'Greta,' she said firmly. 'I want to accept your invitation, but I have a great favour to ask. I want to come now, at once. I want to come and use you as a base for walking trips, yes, all summer, a long time . . . And I don't want anyone to know where I am. I don't want James to know. Or Rose. Not anyone. All right? Yes, I'll ring you from Oslo.'

There, it was done.

She briskly began to collect the clothes she would need.

Tomorrow she would put her home into the hands of an estate agent, and go at once to the airport.

Tonight, now, she would go out to dinner at a restaurant, not come home until late, and she would not answer the telephone . . . which was ringing as she ran down the stairs away from it.

What Price the Truth?

I want to tell you something, I have to tell *someone*. *I have
to talk*. I suddenly understood you are the only person
left who will know what I'm talking about. Has that
happened to you? You suddenly think, My God, that was
twenty, thirty years ago and I am the only person left who
knows what really happened?

Do you remember Caesar? Remember I worked for him?
Do you – most people have forgotten. We called him Caesar
. . . he never knew it of course. Because he used to say, I'm
going to conquer Britain – remember that? If you do, then
you and I are the only people left who do. Well, Caesar's
son married my daughter last weekend . . . yes, exactly, you
can't improve on life, can you, Life: God's little script
writer. But you only know the half of it, *listen*.

Did you ever meet Robert, Caesar's son? If you did, he
must have been an infant. Well, he's turned out a charming
boy, sweet, but really, really nice.

Ten years ago he rang me at the office and asked me out
to dinner. He was fourteen. I was struck dumb. Well, as far
as I can be struck dumb. I was so *tickled* – of course I said
yes. But wait until you hear where. It was at the Berengaria.
Yes, quite so. I don't know what I expected, but he did it all
perfectly. He might have been thirty-five, this kid, this *baby*

he called for me in a taxi with flowers, in a hired suit. He had booked a table and gone in to discuss it all with the head waiter. The waiters were hovering about like nannies, they were tickled out of their wits, because of this kid and me – of course they knew me for years, I used to go there with Caesar, or I went in to arrange special dinners for him. He used to talk as if it was *his* restaurant . . . are you getting the picture? Not by a nod or a beck did the waiters embarrass him, they were wonderful. I sat there going mad with curiosity. *Fourteen*. Then I thought, All right, we are all mad at fourteen, forget it. And I was busy then, as usual. But it must have cost him fifty quid. Where did he get it? Not from his father, that mean old . . .

The next thing, he writes me a letter on best quality ivory vellum notepaper, with his name printed on it, Robert Meredith Stone, asking me to go for a walk in St James's Park, and then tea at the Ritz. Wait a minute, I thought, just wait a minute . . . it's time to do some thinking.

Dinner at the Berengaria fair enough, it was Caesar's place, but a walk in the *park*? Caesar has never set foot off a London pavement. He probably doesn't know a daffodil from a rose. In his old age he sits like a sour old goat grumping at 1930s films on the video, don't imagine he limps about the garden philosophizing while he prunes the roses. Marie has always done the gardening.

I thought it all over, but really *thought*, and then I asked Marie for lunch. I needed to talk to her without Caesar knowing, I didn't want to give poor Robert away.

I hadn't seen Marie for years. We always got on, if you can call it that, having nothing in common but behaving 37 well. She's old these days, she's decided to be an old woman. I'm damned if I will yet. I mean, it's a lot of effort to let yourself get old, you have to change your clothes, your style, everything, it's all right for her, she's got time for all that, she's never had to work in her life. Of course she was curious to know what it was all about and I didn't know how to start. As soon as I saw her I realized I couldn't ask. What was I to say? Tell me, does your Robert think that your Caesar and I had an affair and if so, what's all this about strolls in St James's Park and feeding the ducks?

She thought it was ever so sweet of me to ask her for lunch, but she's got vague, she started to talk about Caesar's girlfriends. 'I never minded,' said she, 'not after the first . . .' And then she made a joke, yes, actually a joke, 'It's the first one that counts, you know, *le premier pas qui coûte*, and he always had such nice women,' paying me a compliment, *noblesse oblige*. 'And I never did like sex,' she says, 'or perhaps I wasn't lucky with Caesar, or he wasn't lucky with me.' I swear she was ready for me to tell her how I had found her Caesar in bed, and I understood something at that moment, it struck me all of a heap, it struck me dumb – yes, all right, but I told you I had to *talk*. Now, this is the point. It was always important to me that I never slept with Caesar, but it was exactly at that moment, eating a healthful salad with Caesar's wife . . . ha ha, how absolutely apropos . . . that I knew how important it was, a point of pride. And now it mattered to her so little she didn't even remember I had gone to her and said, Look here, Marie, I don't know what anyone else thinks and I don't care, but it matters to me what *you* think: I am not sleeping with your husband

and I never did. She didn't remember I had gone specially to tell her. She looked at me vaguely, and said, 'Oh yes? Did you? Funny, I forget things . . . but I don't mind, you know.' She minded all right. She's decided to forget that. Whether she believed me or not she minded like hell and I minded her minding. Because I was innocent. It was just the same having lunch with her as it was *then* – because the one thing I couldn't say was, the most important, your husband is a mean, scrimping, pennywise tightfist, and he's killed me with overwork, he always has to work people he employs to the bone, and he has to underpay them. Never mind about sleeping with me, I would have liked to say, then and at lunch that day, but working with that little Scrooge never left much energy for sex.

Have you forgotten how it was with me then? I had two kids – but *do* you remember? The funny thing is, meeting people in public life, professional life, you meet them as individuals, but what's important about them, often, is what you don't see. In my case it was two small children and an ex-husband who sometimes came through with a few quid but more often didn't. I was being paid a senior typist's wage when I ran Caesar's office for him. I was his Girl Friday, I organized everything, and it was I who had the contacts, I knew everyone in the field when he was a newcomer in it. I used to set up whole shows for him, and he'd take the credit. I used to work from eight in the morning till eleven, twelve, one at night. I made that man and he knew it too, but if he'd paid me, he'd be admitting just what my real worth to him was. I'm not saying he wouldn't have succeeded without me, but if he conquered

Britain – because he did, *we* did, he was known everywhere and not just in this country, he was a name in France and Germany – if he did all that it was because of me. Then one day I was so exhausted I couldn't get out of bed. I telephoned the office and said right, that was it, I was giving him notice, I couldn't stand it. I had to get a job that paid me properly. I was in debt for the rent. I couldn't even pay for the children's clothes, and their father had been out of work for months – he was an actor, it wasn't his fault. Suddenly there is Caesar ringing the doorbell, for the first time, and I'd been working for him ten years then. He comes in, he looks around. Two rooms and a bathroom, oh yes, it was a decent little place, I wasn't going to let the kids go without, but I slept in the living room and they had the other room. 'Nice place,' says Caesar, sniffing about pricing everything, 'you do yourself well.' And he with his bloody great house at Richmond. I got back into bed and actually went to sleep, I was so *ill* I didn't care. 'You can't just give me notice,' he says, waking me up. 'I am giving you notice,' I say. To cut it short, he put up my salary a few quid a month, it was enough to pay off some of my debts. I still wasn't earning as much as a good PR girl. 'You can't leave me,' he says, and I remember the tone of his voice, it was that which struck me dumb, as if *I* had treated *him* badly.

All those years he had been trying to get into bed with me. Particularly when we went on trips. I never would. Partly because I didn't go for him much, and partly because it was a question of self-respect. It was more, it was *survival*. I couldn't let him take me over entirely. He owned my working self, but as for the rest . . . you are still wondering why I stayed with him? I remember you asked me, why stay with him, when you could earn four times the salary? The point is – I fitted that job of his like a . . . I and the job had grown up together . . . I had *made* that job, made him. He knew I wouldn't be able to give it up. He knew that in some funny way we stood and fell together . . . we matched, his talents and mine, we were a team. But he got rich, did you know? He was a millionaire. Typically he used to say, what's a million these days? And I wasn't going to say, If it's nothing, then give me a little of it. *Pride.* Okay, okay, sometimes I do wonder about that . . . but I think what I felt was, if I can stand this I can stand anything. I felt strong . . . I felt indestructible.

You did think I slept with him, didn't you? Everyone did. He made sure everyone did. He'd speak of me in a certain way, he'd put on that smile . . . if there was a big do, a first night or something, he'd take me in on his arm, and make sure everyone noticed. Caesar and his mistress. I went along with it, but I'd give him a look – and he understood all right. It was a battle, a fight to the death. I was saying, All right, but you and I know the truth. I'm not your woman and never shall be.

That went on for years. And then they offered me the job I have now and that coincided with Caesar deciding he'd had enough, time to put his feet up.

And all these years I've been thinking, you old goat, you little gauleiter, but I never slept with you.

And there I was sitting opposite old Marie and suddenly I realized she had forgotten all about it and didn't care. And that made me feel . . . I felt that I was collapsing inside, 41 somewhere. It had been so important to me.

But at least during the lunch I understood what had happened ... his kids were still small when I finished working for Caesar. But as they grew up they would hear him talking about me, in that proprietary way of his. Robert would have got the idea. Meanwhile I was going from strength to strength. I'm very *visible*, you know. When I was working for him it was one thing – everyone had to think his Girl Friday slept with him. But for a long time now he'd have good reason to boast about me. If you are wondering, But where did Robert get the idea about little walks in the park and tea at the Ritz, well, God knows. But he's a dear sweet lovely boy, he's nice, I mean nice in himself, he's a romantic, and so he would think that little strolls in the park and tea at the Ritz are part of the perfect love affair.

He wrote me love letters. He obviously copied them from some pattern letters. Or perhaps he got them out of a novel. I was absolutely *wowed* by them, they were like something from the eighteenth century, well perhaps they were. I'd wait a few days and then send him a couple of tickets to a play or a first night. I'd see him there with a girl, and then it was with my daughter Sonia. Do you remember her? She's beautiful. Yes, all right I can say it now ... she's like me when I was young. And *that* is the point.

Robert started taking her out regularly. I thought nothing of it. I was *busy*. I've only just realized how hard I've worked. Why did I have to, what is it all about, okay, I had to work myself silly when I had to support the children, but even when they are off my hands ... if you can call it that, none of them are ever off our hands these days, but at least they wouldn't starve if you said, enough, that's it, I've had it, don't expect any more from me – do you know one reason I would never say that? Because I wouldn't want to be as mean as Caesar, that's why.

Then, about a year ago, Marie rings me, worldly-wise, you know, and she says, 'What do you think about our Robert and your Sonia? They're getting married. We told him, you are too young, but of course none of them listen.'

I'm sure you've already worked it all out. Robert has always wanted to be Caesar the Second. *But.* He's not ambitious, you see. He doesn't know what ambition is. He works nicely in that advertising office, and dreams about being Caesar, but he doesn't make the connection some-where . . . you need to kill yourself working, or get someone else to kill themselves working for you . . . he's too nice to be successful, do you see? But if he can get his father's mistress then he's half-way there.

Are you wondering how much of this my Sonia sees? Not much. She thinks I was Caesar's mistress and hates me for it. Once I said to her, Sonia, you two children and I were stuck together in two rooms until you were twenty. You know I didn't have men – where would I have put them? What about those trips, she says, catching me out. I said Sonia, I was so tired every night often enough I used to fall into bed with all my clothes on . . . well, actually I did have the occasional little fling, when I had the energy, which wasn't often. But that was nothing to do with her. I understood something . . . she's never worked hard in her life. She doesn't know what working hard means. She doesn't know what it means being so tired you're scared to even let go half an inch, because if you did everything would fall to pieces. And she will never know because Robert looks after her like a precious kitten that will never grow up. He must think that is how his father looked after me. He's so decent that it would never enter his head to think otherwise. Caesar was a sweet kind father-figure, and so that's what he's going to be too.

To cut it short . . .

The wedding was last Saturday. We had six hundred guests. All of show business, television, radio, theatre, everything, on Caesar's side a bit reminiscent, because he's been retired for so long.

And there *we* were, Marie, mother of the bridegroom, Caesar, father of the bridegroom, Sonia's daddy – but he's always been a bit noises-off, not that it's his fault, and me, mother of the bride.

And when it came to photographs . . . no, wait, here's the nitty-gritty. Robert suddenly came forward and took charge. Suddenly I saw him as Caesar. Do you remember that deadly quiet bloody-mindedness, that determination, smiling all the time but no one was going to get in his way? That was Robert, all of last Saturday afternoon. It was absolutely essential he get a photograph of himself and Sonia, with me and Caesar standing on either side, and then a picture of us standing behind them, and then sitting in front – and so on, over and over. It was embarrassing. Daddy and his famous mistress, and Daddy's son and the mistress as she used to be. All afternoon people were saying to me. God *darling*, but your daughter's *exactly* as you used to look.

Well, I kept giving Caesar looks, the way I used to, but he didn't know what was going on. I swear when some men retire they just give up all their *nous* – I swear, in the old days, he would have seen it all, even if he wouldn't admit it. What he did *not* see was that all of his *awful* ruthless single-mindedness, I came, I saw, I conquered, was there in his son, but focused on just one pathetic thing, that he should marry daddy's mistress.

And I felt more and more . . . that I didn't exist. Do you understand?

Well. It was ever such a *gemütlich* ceremony, it was a wonderful party, a good time was had by all, and when the happy couple went off to Venice, my treat, my daughter gave me a look of pure triumph, though God knows what she thinks she's triumphing about. And he, that *sweet* boy, he kissed me, the sort of kiss a lover gives you, goodbye for ever.

And the point is, this is the point, this is the absolutely *bloody* point . . . there is no way I could ever say to anyone, and I hardly dare think it, in case I come out with it by mistake, no, I was not Caesar's mistress, never, I never so much as kissed him, because that would be the whole basis of that sweet boy's life *gone*. The whole thing – focusing on Sonia, cutting out all her other suitors, marrying her publicly in front of his father's world and mine, treating the girl like a prize puppy – all *nothing*, based on nothing at all.

Nada.

And there's no one I can talk to about it, no one I can tell . . . except you. Well, darling, do the same for you some time. 45

Two Old Women and a Young One

The restaurant is used by publishers, by agents, and – if guests of one or the other – by authors. About the restaurant nothing much can be said: it is yet to be explained why one restaurant is more popular than another whose food is also adequate. It was perhaps too interestingly decorated, but at the same time it aspired to opulence. It is always full.

Midday. People were arriving for lunch. By themselves at a favoured table beside a cascade of cream-and-green ivies were two old women. They were smartly dressed but fussily, with scarves, necklaces, earrings. Actresses? Was there a suggestion of self-parody in those eyelashes, the eye paint?

They sat catercornered. Their table was set for a third. They refused an aperitif, then, as the restaurant went on filling, they asked for sherries.

'Very dry,' said one, to the waiter, and the voice announced that she was older than she seemed, for it wavered.

'Very dry,' said the other, a good octave lower, in a voice once pitched to be sexy, but now it rumbled on the edge of a croak.

'Very good,' said the waiter, and he lingered a moment.

smiling. He was a lively young Frenchman.

'Perhaps we have the wrong day?' remarked one.

'I am sure we have not,' said the other.

And here came their host, a youngish man almost running to them, blank-eyed with anxiety. 'I'm so sorry,' he as good as wept, and ran his hand back over his boyish hair, disordered as it was by apology and by haste. He sat and the same waiter nodded, as he called, 'Champagne, the usual.'

'Dear me,' said one old woman, 'we are being spoiled.' She was, perhaps, the prettier, a delightful old thing. Younger she must have been delightful, a rose, blue-eyed, blonde, and her hair even now was silver, a mass of intricate waves, tendrils, not unlike the casque favoured by old Queen Mary.

'Indeed we are,' said the other in her deep voice. She had certainly been striking, with dark eyes and, probably, hair. Now it was gold, a pale gold, in a modified chignon, held with a black velvet bow.

Sisters?

'I was held up on your account – not that it's an excuse,' said the host, and reached for the just-filled champagne glass. He waited only long enough for politeness, for as the other two glasses began to bubble and bead he swallowed down his first glass and at once the waiter refilled it. The two women watched and exchanged the briefest glance.

'It's all sorted out,' said the publisher. 'There will be two contracts, both on the same terms. It is being assumed you two will contribute equally to the book.'

'Oh, good,' said silver-hair. 'Well, that's agreed, then. I'm so glad.' And she put back her champagne, in a gulp, 47 and smiled gently at him.

'Of course,' said gold-head, in her throaty voice. 'I was sure you'd sort it all out.' And she, too, drank off her glass.

'How nice,' said silver-hair, 'to drink champagne at lunchtime.' Her voice was already more quavery than it had been, and when it reached for lower notes it achieved a reminiscent intimacy.

'How nice,' said gold-head, 'to drink champagne with a handsome young man.'

'Oh come on,' said he, bluffly, startled. Quite upset he was. William was his name: call-me-William, but he wouldn't say this to these two who, it was obvious, would take advantage in some way.

The two women were focusing on him an inspection that he experienced as an intrusion. He was saying to himself, in a moment of panic, that between them they claimed almost a century and a half of years.

He sat staring over his champagne glass at the two old women. He had not met them before, only spoken on the telephone, and as a result of these talks he had personally overlooked every clause of the contracts. He had not expected . . . well, he was shocked. Nothing in his experience had taught him how to see these two worldly old trouts, now both tight on a couple of swallows of champagne.

'Darling,' said silver-hair, 'we've scared him.' And she put her hand, shapely but blotched with age and full of rings, on his forearm.

48 'Don't mind us,' said gold-head, it seemed to him with a quite grotesque naughtiness, 'but it is all going to our poor

heads.'

Meanwhile the waiter was observing all this. He filled the three glasses.

'We both of us live alone, you see,' said silver-hair, explaining it all to him.

'Oh, I thought you lived together . . . I don't know why I did . . .'

'We may be sisters, but we haven't come to that yet.'

'We're still hoping for something better, you see,' said gold-head, and then gave a snort of derisive laughter, God knows at what.

'Living alone with my baby,' said silver-hair, who in fact was Fanny Winterhome.

'And I live with mine, and we both love our babies,' said gold-head, Kate Bisley.

They were widows. They had been theatrical agents for thirty years, had known 'everybody', had represented a thousand good troupers, famous and less famous, and now they were writing their reminiscences. The book would certainly sell for its anecdotes about the great, pretty near the bone some of them. 'But never spiteful, darling, we promise you,' Fanny had assured him on the telephone. There was also the question of their theatre expertise, past and present. No one knew more than they did, he had been assured.

Yesterday the young (youngish) publisher had been told, quite by chance, by a well-known actor he had asked to help 'promote' the book, that the two women had been beautiful.

He sat looking from one to the other.

'Kate has a Burmese, and my baby is a Siamese,' said Fanny. And her rouged lips kiss-kissed the air, an invisible pussycat.

'I think we had better order,' he said firmly.

It was evident he cared about what he ate, and they did not. But as the waiter approached to drain the end of the champagne into the three glasses the host said, hypnotized into doing it – he was convinced – 'Another bottle, I think.'

'Oh good,' sighed Fanny. 'One can never have too much champagne.'

'One can at this time of the day,' said Kate.

'Well, we'll have to support each other to the train.'

'Or perhaps this handsome man would escort us there?'

'I certainly would, with pleasure, but I have an appointment I simply cannot be late for.'

'Oh dear, then we mustn't expect too much of you,' Fanny said, patting the pretty silver lattice above her pearl-bubbled left ear while her rings flashed. A ring caught in the hair. 'Oh damn,' she said, 'I've got out of the way of dolling myself up.' And she unclipped the earring, laid it on the cloth, unclipped the other, took off a ring or two.

'It was all for you,' said Kate, 'but we are out of practice, you see.' She was offering herself to him in the tones of her deep voice, just as Fanny did her light one. Their voices . . . while he smiled and tucked heartily into his starter, prawns and bits of this and that, he was trying to come to terms with their voices.

'Aren't you even going to ask about the terms?' he enquired, whimsically, but with an undernote of grudge.

'Oh I'm sure you've done well by us,' said Fanny, her

voice tinkling down with his spine.

'Besides, you wrote us the terms, have you forgotten?' said Kate, and her deep bell made a descant with Fanny's chime.

Damn them, he was thinking.

'Besides, it's not likely you would try to cheat us,' said Fanny, 'when we were the best agents in the business in our time.'

'True,' he said.

Both, having allowed the tines of their forks to dawdle in their fish, put down the forks and reached as one woman for their glasses.

'Bliss,' said Fanny, sipping.

'Bliss plus,' echoed Kate.

He was looking past them at a table visible through a slight arch, where sat a young woman, who was facing him. She was entertaining an influential New York publisher, and was not looking at him, though she must have seen him there. She was more attractive, in style not unlike the Modigliani we all know so well. She had a long voluptuous white throat. Her black hair glistened like clean coal, and was cut in what was once called a bob. She had green eyes, and wore a grass-green jumper with a string of jet beads. Her skin was white, with the thick glistening look of camellia petals. He certainly was not the only man looking at her. But she had eyes only for the man opposite her, attending to him like . . . well, like a mistress determined to please. He acknowledged that it would not have occurred to him to make this comparison if he had not been subjected to these two old . . .

As she continued not to acknowledge him, he leaned back again, prepared to put up with being embarrassed.

They had noticed his absence of mind, and sat as quiet as two pampered budgies, drinking, musing, it seemed, about long-ago things – attractive memories, for their wrinkled mouths smiled, and their eyes were damp with champagne.

He began on his main course, while they patiently, but indifferently, waited for him. They had said they didn't want a main course. Urged again now to change their minds, Fanny said, 'The pudding! That's what I'm waiting for. I adore, adore sweet things now. I never used to.'

'Sweets to the sweet,' said Kate, apparently complimenting Fanny for him, since it didn't occur to him to do so. Or was this a moment from her own past?

Both were now quite tipsy, and Kate actually swayed a little, and unsteadily hummed a bar or two of – what?

Fanny put her head on one side, lips pursed, and Kate said triumphantly, 'I've Got You Under My Skin.'

'What a tune to dance to, that was,' said Fanny. 'Do you dance?' she enquired, caressing him with her old sweet voice.

'No, they don't dance these days,' said Kate. 'We danced. They none of them do. Not real dancing. They just jump about.'

'No,' he confessed, fortifying himself with champagne. 'I don't actually ever seem to . . .'

The second bottle was almost gone. No, he simply would not, he was damned if he would, order a third.

He had swallowed down his food, and had not enjoyed it.

52   He nodded, and knew it was desperate, at the waiter,

who, it was obvious, knew exactly how to deal with these *monstres sacrées*. He came gracefully forward, smiling, bestowing his attention on both, in friendly glances, and began detailed explanations of the desserts. He might have been describing jewels, or orchids. His manner was full of flattery, and of appreciation, of the food, and certainly, of them. He had a favourite granny perhaps? The three were positively flirting! It was quite charming, as a performance, the host was prepared to concede that. When it was finally agreed that a certain confection of chocolate and *crème fraîche* was what they had to eat, the waiter pointed out it was not wise to let all those pretty things – for both women had now made piles of jewellery beside them – lie about anyhow on the tablecloth. He smiled, they smiled, and both swept up their valuables and let them fall into their handbags.

'How do you know I wouldn't run off with them myself?' enquired the waiter laughing, departing to fetch their desserts.

'Oh don't be silly,' sighed Kate after him.

'He's a dish,' said Fanny. 'I'm sure there are more good-looking young men about than there used to be.'

'An illusion,' said Kate.

They seemed to have forgotten him, or had given him up, for they sat meditating and not looking anywhere near him.

They ate their confections in lingering, appreciative licks and sips, but no, this performance was not meant for him, the host, who sat watching, trying to see them as the waiter clearly did, charming women, for when he had an unoccupied moment, he stood nearby, smilingly watching.

Last week a certain impresario had remarked that these two had been the dishiest women in London.

Dishy. A dish. Dishes. Dishiest.

The champagne was quite gone.

No, neither drank coffee these days and brandy would be too much of a good thing. They were quite happy to toddle off to their train.

He told the waiter he would be back to pay the bill, and he took them out, one on either arm. This contact disturbed him, but he did not propose to analyse why. The waiter was holding the door open, 'Au revoir, au revoir,' he said. 'Come back, madame, do come back, madame.'

And, before turning back to his duties, he stood looking after them, and gave the minutest shrug, regretful, philosophic, humorously tender.

There was a taxi almost at once. The host handed them in, both slightly unsteady, but in command of themselves. As he bent to smile goodbye, it occurred to him they were actually saying to themselves, and would to each other the moment he had turned away, 'Right, we've got that over.' A performance was done with. The very second their little waves at him – which seemed to him perfunctory, to say the least – were done with, they sat back and forgot him.

He returned to the restaurant. Now the Modigliani girl was alone. He sat himself down at her table, just as another colleague did. The three of them worked in different departments of the same publishing firm.

'God,' said she, 'what one has to do for duty.' She smiled matily at first one and then the other, but holding their eyes with hers. An Armagnac stood before her. She was a little tight too. 'Drinking at lunchtime,' she complained.

At the next table sat a woman they all knew, an American agent in London. She greeted them, they greeted her, and she began to talk about her trip, enquiring about new young writers. Her voice resonated, commanded attention, as American professional women's voices often do, insistent, not conceding an inch, every syllable a claim.

The Modigliani girl answered her, and her voice was just as much in a local pattern as the American's. Somewhere in England, at a girls' school, at some time probably in the late sixties or early seventies, there must have been a headmistress, or even a head girl, of extreme force of character, or elegant, or rich, or pretty, but at least with some quality that enabled her to impose her style on everyone, making her enviable, copiable ... by a class – then a school – then by several. For often and everywhere is to be found this voice among professional women formed at that time. It is a little breathy high voice that comes from a circumscribed part of the women who use it, not more than two square inches of the upper chest, certainly not a chest cavity or resonating around a head. Oh dear, poor little me, they lisp their appeals to the unkind world; these tough, often ruthless young women who use every bit of advantage they can. Sometimes in a restaurant this voice can be heard from more than one of the tables; or from different parts of a room at a board meeting, or a conference. There they sat, in professional and competent discussion, the American tough guy, the English cutie, or sweetie, or dish, or dolly-face, perfect specimens of their kind, one insisting and grinding, one chitter-chattering, and smiling, turning her beautiful long white neck, curved and taut, while the black silky hair swung on her cheeks.

Two men watched and listened.

Then their girl, their colleague, turned her attention back to them. 'I'm going to play hookey this afternoon. I'm not coming back to my office,' she almost whispered, and her great emerald eyes widened like a little girl's at the dark. 'I want to get home and feed my baby. I've got myself a new friend, he's a baby chow, he's a little love . . .'

The waiter brought the old women's host his bill: he checked and signed.

Brought the beauty her bill: she signed having given it a fast cold inspection a million miles from this whispering confiding style, but reminded her colleagues of the sharpness she used in her work. Meanwhile she lisped, 'My life has changed. When Bill and I parted . . .' Bill was her recently divorced husband . . . 'I thought that was really it you know, for ever, absolutely the *end* for me, but now have my baby-love, I've lost my heart again. He sleeps on my bed, I try to keep him off, I've made him a little little nest on the floor – he's only the size of a big teddy, you know, but he won't have it . . .' She smiled at them, breaking their hearts.

All three should be back in the office, should have left here half an hour ago, should at least be leaving now, but she held them there: 'I take him out, I take my baby to the park every morning before I come to work, yes, it's a discipline, just like a real baby, and when I take him home give him some little things to play with while I'm gone, he loves to play with green leaves or a twig. Oh he's so pretty dancing about in the grass, he's like a baby lion . . .'

They sat on, and would until she broke it, got up to go, abandoned them.

But if they could not get up and leave her, then it seemed she could not end the business of charming them . . .

A Note on Doris Lessing

Doris Lessing was born in Persia of British parents in 1919. She spent her childhood on her father's farm in what was then Southern Rhodesia. After leaving school at 14 she worked in a variety of jobs including typist, au pair and telephonist, maintaining her interest in writing all the while. Upon arrival in England in 1949 her first novel *The Grass is Singing* was published (and was subsequently filmed in 1981). In 1952 the publishing of *Martha Quest* marked the first in her famous sequence of five novels *Children of Violence* which ended with *The Four-Gated City* (1969).

Ms Lessing's collection of short novels called *Five* earned her the Somerset Maugham Award for 1954 and her play *Play With a Tiger* was presented in the West End in 1962. The French translation of *The Golden Notebook* (1962) won the Prix Medici in 1976. In 1982 she received the Austrian State Prize for Literature and the Shakespeare Prize, Hamburg. Doris Lessing has been shortlisted for the Booker Prize three times: *Briefing for a Descent Into Hell* (1971), *The Sirian Experiments* (1981) and *The Good Terrorist* (1985) and won the W. H. Smith Award in 1985. Doris Lessing's interests include politics, literature music, art and religion. Her books have been translated into many languages. She lives in London.